DALE, DALE, DALE
Una fiesta de números
HIT IT, HIT IT, HIT IT
A Fiesta of Numbers

By/Por
René Saldaña, Jr.

Illustrations by/Ilustraciones de
Carolyn Dee Flores

Piñata Books
Arte Público Press
Houston, Texas

Publication of *Dale, dale, dale: Una fiesta de números / Hit It, Hit It, Hit It: A Fiesta of Numbers* is funded by a grant from the City of Houston through the Houston Arts Alliance. We are grateful for their support.

Piñata Books are full of surprises!

Piñata Books
An Imprint of Arte Público Press
University of Houston
4902 Gulf Fwy, Bldg 19, Rm 100
Houston, Texas 77204-2004

Cover design by Mora Des!gn

Saldaña, Jr., René.
    Dale, dale, dale : una fiesta de números / by René Saldaña, Jr. ; ilustraciones de Carolyn Dee Flores = Hit it, hit it, hit it : a fiesta of numbers / by René Saldaña, Jr. ; illustrations by Carolyn Dee Flores.
        p. cm.
    Summary: "In this bilingual counting picture book, a young boy counts to fourteen in anticipation of his birthday party: one piñata filled with candy; two hours until the party; three tables set for all of the guests, etc."—Provided by publisher.
    ISBN 978-1-55885-782-7 (alk. paper)
    [1. Birthdays—Fiction. 2. Parties—Fiction. 3. Counting. 4. Spanish language materials—Bilingual.] I. Flores, Carolyn Dee, illustrator. II. Title. III. Title: Hit it, hit it, hit it.
PZ73.S27416 2014
[E]—dc23
                                                                              2013037331
                                                                                     CIP

∞ The paper used in this publication meets the requirements of the American National Standard for Permanence of Paper for Printed Library Materials Z39.48-1984.

Printed in Hong Kong in November 2013–February 2014 by Book Art Inc. / Paramount Printing Company Limited.
12 11 10 9 8 7 6 5 4 3 2 1

Para Tina, Lukas, Mikah, Jakob, y Kalyn.
—RSJ

Para mis tías Alice y Rara, y en memoria de mi tía Eudie.
—CDF

For Tina, Lukas, Mikah, Jakob, and Kalyn.
—RSJ

For my aunts Alice and Rara, and in memory of my aunt Eudie.
—CDF

Hoy es mi cumpleaños, y estoy muy ansioso.

Today is my birthday, and I am so excited.

Una piñata llena de dulces.

One piñata filled with candy.

Dos horas para que empiece la fiesta.

Two hours until the party.

Tres mesas listas para todos los invitados.

Three tables set for all of the children.

Cuatro cajas llenas de regalitos para todos los niños. Pero, qué otras sorpresas encontraremos . . .

Four boxes filled with gifts for the guests. But, what other surprises will we find . . .

cinco máscaras de la lucha libre,

five wrestling masks,

seis trompos,

six tops,

siete botellitas de burbujas,

seven bottles with bubbles,

ocho bolsitas llenas de canicas,

eight bags filled with marbles,

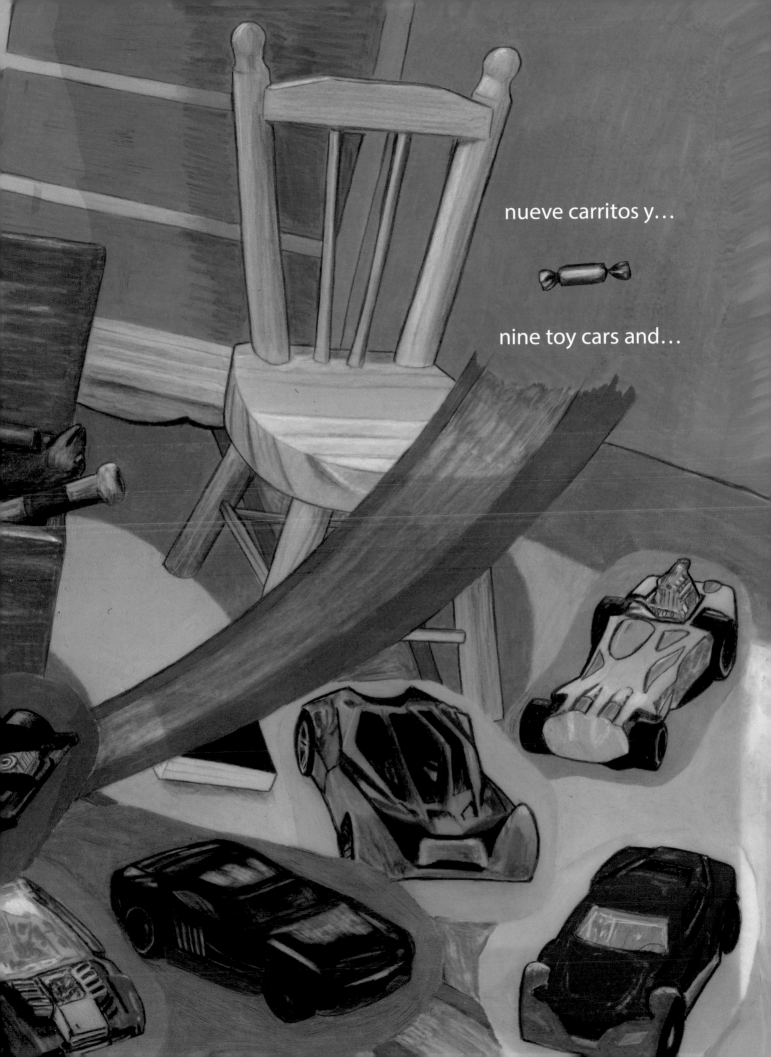

diez guitarritas para tocar y cantar. Y ahora,
a comer pastel y cantar una canción.

ten little guitars to strum
while we sing. And now,
let's eat cake and sing a
song.

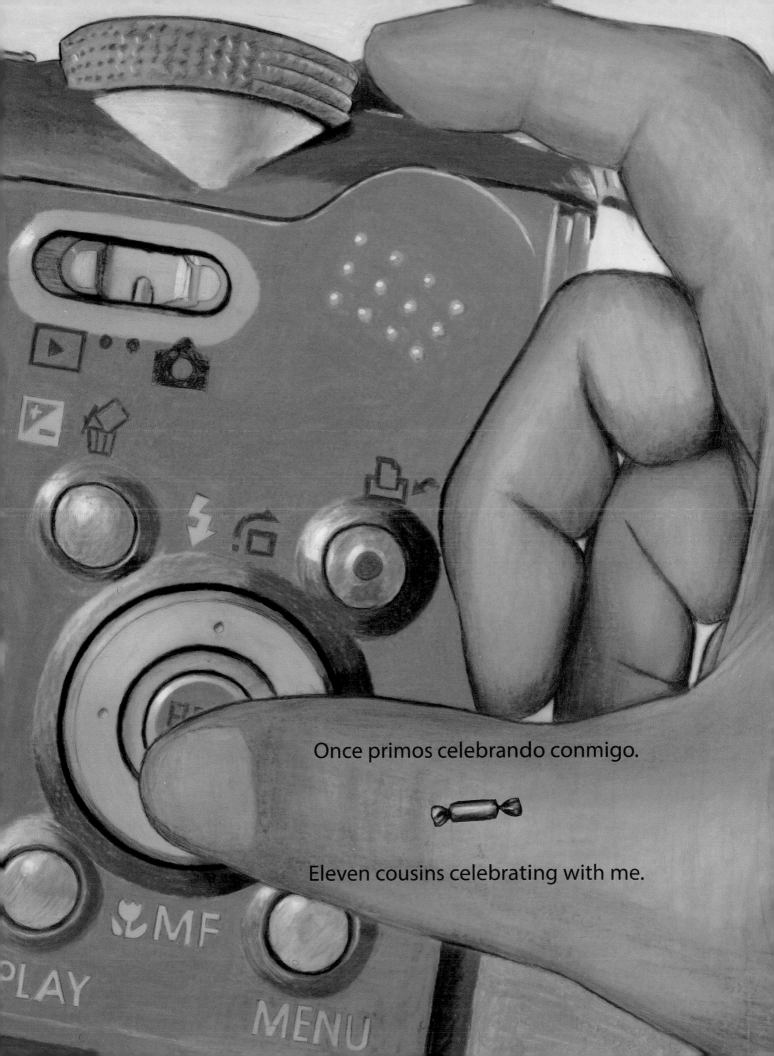

Once primos celebrando conmigo.

Eleven cousins celebrating with me.

Doce niños listos para
darle a la piñata.

Dale, dale, dale,
no pierdas el tino;
porque si lo pierdes
pierdes el camino.
Ya le diste una,
ya le diste dos;
ya le diste tres,
y tu tiempo se acabó.

Twelve children ready to
swing at the piñata.

Hit it, hit it, hit it,
don't dare lose your aim,
because if you do lose it
you shall lose your way.
You have hit it one time,
you have hit it twice,
now you've hit it three times,
and your turn is up.

¡Y yo, el primero, el niño más feliz
en todo el mundo!

And I get to go first, the happiest
boy in the whole wide world!

René Saldaña, Jr. lives and teaches in Lubbock, Texas. He is the author of several books for young readers, including the bilingual Mickey Rangel mystery series, *A Good Long Way, Dancing with the Devil and Other Stories from Beyond / Bailando con el diablo y otros cuentos del más allá* and *The Jumping Tree*. He has celebrated more than his share of birthdays and broken enough piñatas that he's stopped having them for himself, but he loves throwing fiestas for his children, Lukas, Mikah, Kalyn and Jakob. And his wife, Tina, plans the best birthday parties ever!

René Saldaña, Jr. vive y trabaja en Lubbock, Texas. Es autor de varios libros juveniles, incluyendo la colección bilingüe Mickey Rangel, Detective Privado, *A Good Long Way, Dancing with the Devil and Other Stories from Beyond / Bailando con el diablo y otros cuentos del más allá* y *The Jumping Tree*. Ha celebrado y compartido tantos cumpleaños y quebrado tantas piñatas que ya ha dejado de hacerlo para sí mismo, pero le encanta hacerles fiestas a sus hijos, Lukas, Mikah, Kalyn y Jakob. Y su esposa, Tina, ¡organiza las mejores fiestas de cumpleaños!

Carolyn Dee Flores attended Trinity University and worked as a computer analyst before becoming a professional rock musician and composer. She wrote soundtracks for independent and educational films, T.V. and commercials— and then, became a children's illustrator. Carolyn illustrated *Canta, Rana, canta / Sing, Froggie, Sing* (Piñata Books, 2013) and *Daughters of Two Nations* (Mountain Press Publishing Company, 2013). Carolyn's original artwork can be found in the permanent collection of the Mazza Museum and at the Arne Nixon Center for the Study of Children's Literature. She is a member of the Society of Children's Book Writers and Illustrators.

Carolyn Dee Flores estudió en Trinity University y trabajó como analista de sistemas antes de convertirse en músico de rock profesional y compositora. Escribió música para films independientes y educacionales, televisión y comerciales —y luego, se convirtió en ilustradora de libros infantiles. Carolyn ilustró *Canta, Rana, canta / Sing, Froggie, Sing* (Piñata Books 2013) y *Daughters of Two Nations* (Mountain Press Publishing Company, 2013). La obra de Carolyn se encuentra en la colección permanente del Mazza Museum y en el Arne Nixon Center for the Study of Children's Literature. Carolyn es miembro del Society of Children's Book Writers and Illustrators.